Easily Confused Words
易混淆詞

Aman Chiu 著

新雅文化事業有限公司
www.sunya.com.hk

本書主題

全書以易混淆詞為主題，共有60個單元，囊括小學生經常容易混淆的 60 組英文字詞，內容多元豐富、實用有趣，助學童提升英語能力！

形近字詞
4 adapt vs adopt

形近字詞分清楚

詞語辨析

adapt（拼寫中間是 a）解作「適應」，作不及物動詞用；也可解作「使……適應；改動；改編；改造」，作及物動詞用。

adopt（拼寫中間是 o）解作「領養（孩子或寵物）」，可作及物或不及物動詞用。

adapt 讀作 /əˈdæpt/，adopt 則讀作 /əˈdɒpt/。

例句示範

adapt
- The children have adapted to their new school.
  孩子已經適應了新學校。
- They want to adapt the novel for television.
  他們想把這部小說改編成電視劇。

adopt
- She was adopted when she was three. 她三歲時被人收養。
- The couple hope to adopt. 那對夫婦希望領養孩子。

增潤知識

adapt 解作「適應」時，常在受詞後加上 to 來連接名詞或原型動詞。例如：
- He can't adapt to the new job. 他適應不了新工作。

adapt 作及物動詞用時，很多時候會以被動句式出現。例如：
- The toilet is adapted for blind people to use.
  這個廁所改裝成適合盲人使用。
- This novel has been adapted for children.
  這部小說改編成兒童故事。

漫畫看一看

每個單元均有一組重點詞目，由趣味漫畫帶出一對易混淆詞，孩子可從具體情境中學懂分辨易混淆詞，增添閱讀樂趣，成效事半功倍。

形近 / 同音 / 意近字詞分清楚

本書把易混淆詞劃分三大類別：形近字詞、同音字詞、意近字詞。各類別的詞目均有深入淺出的文字解說，包括3個欄目：

❶ 詞語辨析
❷ 例句示範
❸ 增潤知識

① 🔍 詞語辨析

從拼寫、含義、用法多方面着手，對比各組易混淆詞，剖析學習要點，助學生輕鬆區別易混淆詞。形近字詞及同音字詞更附音標，以便學童掌握發音。

② ⭐ 例句示範

收錄地道實用的雙語例句，示範詞彙如何正確使用，並鼓勵孩子吸收學習，模仿應用，多讀多寫。

③ 🔍 增潤知識

提供語法、句構、相反詞、同義詞、慣用語等語言知識，全面培養孩子的英文語感，從此不再誤用易混淆詞。

同音字詞分清楚

🔍 詞語辨析

principal（拼寫結尾是 pal）作名詞用時，指「校長」；作形容詞用時，指「主要的；最重要的」。

principle（拼寫結尾是 ple）作名詞用，指「原理；原則」或「道德原則；（行為）準則」。

principal 和 principle 發音相同，都讀作 /ˈprɪn.sə.pᵊl/。

⭐ 例句示範

principal

- This is just a small school with five teachers and a principal.
  這是一間小學校，只有五名教師和一名校長。
- What is your principal reason for taking singing lessons?
  你上唱歌班的主要原因是什麼？
- The principal character in the story is a mermaid.
  這個故事的主角是一條美人魚。

principle

- The basic principle is that all children have the right to education. 基本原則是所有兒童都有接受教育的權利。
- It's against my principles to tell lies. 說謊有違我的原則。

🔍 增潤知識

在美式英語，principal 指中小學的校長。但在英式英語，principal 指大學或學院的校長；中小學的校長一般叫 headteacher。

慣用語 in principle 指「原則上；基本上」。例如：

- They have accepted our proposal in principle.
  他們基本上已經接受了我們的建議書。

87

練習室

書末附設6個練習，涵蓋書中所學，動動腦筋，鞏固知識，自我檢測學習成果。

練習室 1 🏆

There is a mistake in each of the following sentences. Strike them through and correct them in the spaces provided.

下列句子均有一處錯版，請畫去錯版的部分，並在橫線上寫上正確答案。

範例	Uncle Pang is very high.	tall
①	Lie the pens on the table, please.	
②	This skirt suits you perfectly.	
③	This reservoir has fewer water than that one.	
④	Everyone was invited to the party accept Mary.	
⑤	Do you play other sports beside badminton?	
⑥	Would you like some desert?	
⑦	Could you take me some water?	
⑧	I lent a novel from the library yesterday.	
⑨	Its so nice of you to invite us!	
⑩	My bag was opened and my wallet was gone!	

答案：1. Lie → Lay 2. suits → fit 3. fewer → less 4. accept → except 5. beside → besides 6. desert → dessert 7. take → bring 8. lent → borrowed 9. Its → It's 10. opened → open

130

練習室 2 🏆

Fill in the blanks with the correct word for the following sentences. Change the word form if necessary.

請為下列句子填寫正確的字詞，並按需改變字詞的開形。

範例	adapt / adopt
	They've ___adopted___ a baby boy.
	It took me a while to ___adapt___ to the new job.

waist / waste
1a. What a complete _____ of time!
1b. The jeans are too tight around my _____.

flea / flee
2a. Many people have _____ their homes because of war.
2b. Are you sure the kitten has _____?

sweat / sweet
3a. We were dripping with _____ after running.
3b. She bought a packet of _____.

aisle / isle
4a. Would you prefer a window or an _____ seat?
4b. Can you find _____ of Wight on the map?

pray / prey
5a. Let's _____ for the victims of the earthquake.
5b. The tiger is stalking its _____.

答案：1a. waste 1b. waist 2a. fled 2b. fled 3a. sweat 3b. sweets 4a. aisle 4b. Isle 5a. pray 5b. prey

131

作者的話

　　英語詞彙極其豐富，單是常用字就數以千計，加上形、音、義相近或相同的字詞多不勝數，如不仔細分辨，就很容易出錯，出現張冠李戴的情況。事實上，英語中有些單詞驟眼看沒有分別，容易令人混淆，甚至連英語母語人士都會誤用，這是因為英語源自許多不同的語言和方言。

　　其中，有些詞語的拼寫十分相似，甚至只是一字之差，用法和意思卻是南轅北轍，如：aboard 和 abroad。有些發音完全相同，拼寫卻有分別，用法和意思也有天壤之別，如：die 和 dye。有些則是一詞多義，即一個詞語包含多種意思，如 lift 一字，既指「電梯」（名詞），也指「舉起」（動詞）。另外，有些是多詞一義，即不同的詞語指向同一個意思，如：autumn 和 fall，都指「秋天」。換句話說，如果我們只死背一個相對的中文詞義，那麼就會出現偏差。

　　學習英語時，我們特別需要注意形似詞（即拼寫相似的字詞），因為它們往往在閱讀時給我們造成困惑，而且在測驗或考試的詞彙選題或填充題中，也會出現形似詞作為干擾，我們稍不留神就容易出錯。

本書專門辨析詞義和用法容易混淆的英語字詞，並有以下四大特色：

　　第一，全書 60 課，共收錄 60 組易混淆詞，對其含義和用法進行了系統的對比和解釋。

　　第二，所有收錄在本書內的易混淆詞均配有例句，展示正確用法，所舉示例能幫助讀者有效識別詞語之間的差異。

　　第三，每課還附有用法説明，闡釋特殊語法難點，並提供相關語言知識，或介紹相關的同反義詞。

　　第四，書後附設 6 個練習，以供讀者自行測試，鞏固所學。

Aman Chiu

什麼是易混淆詞？
What are easily confused words?

　　易混淆詞是指形（拼寫）、音（發音）、義（意義）相近，容易令人混淆的英文字詞，可細分為以下三類：

一）形近易混淆詞

　　又稱「形似詞」，即拼寫相似的字詞，通常也是音近，所以又稱「近音近形詞」。例如：

aboard vs abroad	advice vs advise	beside vs besides
breathe vs breath	desert vs dessert	medal vs metal

二）同音易混淆詞

　　又稱「同音異義詞」，即發音完全相同，但意義不同的字詞。例如：

aisle vs isle	brake vs break	die vs dye
flea vs flee	peace vs piece	waist vs waste

三）意近易混淆詞

　　即表面上意思相似，但有仔細分別，用法也有差異的字詞。例如：

alone vs lonely	borrow vs lend	bring vs take
fewer vs less	fit vs suit	high vs tall

　　我們學習英語，必須提升對這些詞語的敏感度，才不至於在選詞上指鹿為馬，在理解上模稜兩可，在用字上左右為難。學習要靠一點一滴的累積，才能達到良好的效果，所以大家需多注意英語單詞這一特點，並在背讀單詞時稍加留心，不糊弄過去，不含糊其辭。

目錄 Contents

形近易混淆詞

同音易混淆詞

❓ 詞語辨析

aboard（拼寫中間是 oar）作副詞或介詞用，指「上船、飛機、火車等」或「在船、飛機、火車上」。

abroad（拼寫中間是 roa）作副詞用，用於動詞後，指「在國外；到國外」。

aboard 發音為 /əˈbɔːd/，abroad 則為 /əˈbrɔːd/。

★ 例句示範

aboard

- The stewardess welcomed us **aboard.**
  那名女空中服務員歡迎我們登機。
- The passengers went **aboard** the ship.
  乘客登船了。

abroad

- Lily decided to study **abroad** after the summer holiday.
  莉莉決定了在暑假後出國讀書。
- Their family always go **abroad** during Christmas.
  他們一家每逢聖誕節都會到國外去。

🔍 增潤知識

board 解作「板」，而字首 a- 有「在……之上」的意思，所以 aboard 就是「在板上面」，例如在船的甲板上，其後引申指在飛機上。

board 本身也可作動詞用，指「登上（船、飛機、火車等）」。例如：

- Passengers should **board** the train now.
  乘客現在該登上火車了。

accept vs except

漫畫看一看

❓ 詞語辨析

accept 作動詞用，指「接受；答應；承認」，及物或不及物均可。

except 作介詞用，指「除了……之外」，可後接名詞、名詞短語、從句或介詞短語。

accept 讀作 /əkˈsept/，except 讀作 /ɪkˈsept/，兩者十分相似，分別只在於第一個音節。

⭐ 例句示範

accept

- Don't **accept** any money from strangers.
  不要接受陌生人的金錢。

- They offered dad a job and he **accepted**.
  他們為爸爸提供工作，爸爸接受了。

except

- Most museums in Hong Kong are open daily **except** Tuesdays.
  除了星期二外，大部分香港的博物館每日都開放。

- Kate won't eat anything **except** fruit and vegetables.
  除了水果和蔬菜外，凱特什麼都不吃。

🔍 增潤知識

accept 也可後接 that 子句。例如：

- The shop manager **accepted that** there had been some mistakes. 商店經理承認出了些差錯。

except 也可説成 except for，同樣後接名詞或名詞短語。例如：

- I like all fruit **except (for)** durians.
  除了榴槤外，我什麼水果都愛吃。

漫畫看一看

形近字詞分清楚

❓ 詞語辨析

accident 是名詞，指「突發事故；意外；不測」，一般為不幸事件，而且會造成損壞或傷亡。

incident 是名詞，指「事件；事情」，通常是不愉快或不尋常的。

accident 發音是 /ˈæk.sɪ.dᵊnt/，incident 則是 /ˈɪn.sɪ.dᵊnt/。

★ 例句示範

accident

- I'm sorry I broke the vase; it was an **accident**.
  對不起，我摔破了花瓶，這是意外。

- Two men were injured in the car **accident** last night.
  兩名男子在昨晚的車禍中受傷。

incident

- The plane landed without **incident**.
  航機着陸，未出事故。

- The novel is based on an actual **incident**.
  這部小說是根據真實事件來創作的。

🔍 增潤知識

慣用語 by accident 指「偶然；意外地」。例如：

- I deleted the file **by accident**.
  我不小心刪掉了檔案。

incident 一字主要用在新聞或正式文體。在日常英語中，一般說 something happened。例如：

- People didn't like him because of **something that happened** (= **an incident**) in his past.
  人們因為他過去發生的一些事情而不喜歡他。

漫畫看一看

❓ 詞語辨析

adapt（拼寫中間是 a）解作「適應」，作不及物動詞用；也可解作「使⋯⋯適應；改動；改編；改造」，作及物動詞用。

adopt（拼寫中間是 o）解作「領養（孩子或寵物）」，可作及物或不及物動詞用。

adapt 讀作 /əˈdæpt/，adopt 則讀作 /əˈdɒpt/。

⭐ 例句示範

adapt

- The children have **adapted** to their new school.
  孩子已經適應了新學校。
- They want to **adapt** the novel for television.
  他們想把這部小說改編成電視劇。

adopt

- She was **adopted** when she was three. 她三歲時被人收養。
- The couple hope to **adopt**. 那對夫婦希望領養孩子。

🔍 增潤知識

adapt 解作「適應」時，常在受詞後加上 to 來連接名詞或原型動詞。例如：

- He can't **adapt to** the new job. 他適應不了新工作。

adapt 作及物動詞用時，很多時候會以被動句式出現。例如：

- The toilet is **adapted** for blind people to use.
  這個廁所改裝成適合盲人使用。
- This novel has been **adapted** for children.
  這部小說改編成兒童故事。

advice vs advise

❓ 詞語辨析

advice（拼寫中間是 c）是名詞，解作「勸告；忠告；意見」。

advise（拼寫中間是 s）是及物動詞，解作「勸告（某人）；向（某人）提供意見」。

advice 發音為 /ədˈvaɪs/，advise 則為 /ədˈvaɪz/，兩者十分相似，只是尾音稍有不同，前者發清輔音 /s/，後者發濁輔音 /z/。

⭐ 例句示範

advice

- They gave me some useful **advice**.
  他們提供了一些有用的建議給我。

- I need some **advice** about my English learning.
  我需要一些有關我在英語學習方面的意見。

advise

- We need someone to **advise** us.
  我們需要有個人給我們出主意。

- The doctor **advised** me to rest for a few days.
  醫生建議我休息幾天。

🔍 增潤知識

advice 是不可數名詞，不要說 an advice 或 two advices。如要表達數量，可在 advice 前面加上量詞。例如：

- Can I give you **a piece of advice**?
  我可以給你一則建議嗎？

- I have **ten pieces of advice** for you.
  我有十則建議給你。

漫畫看一看

形近字詞分清楚

❓ 詞語辨析

affect（拼寫開頭是 a）一般作及物動詞用，解作「影響」，也解作「打動」。

effect（拼寫開頭是 e）一般作名詞用，解作「影響；效果；結果」。

affect 讀作 /əˈfekt/，effect 讀作 /ɪˈfekt/，兩者發音很相似，分別在於第一個音節。

⭐ 例句示範

affect

- The illness **affected** her breathing. 疾病影響她呼吸。
- Tiredness is **affecting** my studies. 疲倦影響我學習。
- We were deeply **affected** by the story.
  我們被那個故事深深打動了。

effect

- Eating too much chocolate can have a bad **effect** on your teeth.
  吃太多巧克力對牙齒會有不良影響。
- The **effect** of not having breakfast is to feel really hungry.
  不吃早餐的後果，是你會感到非常肚餓。
- You have to wait 15 minutes for the medicine to take **effect**.
  藥力在 15 分鐘後才發揮效用。

🔍 增潤知識

在美式英語，affect 和 effect 的發音完全相同，都讀作 /əˈfekt/。

短語 side effect 指「副作用」。例如：

- Does this medicine has any **side effects**?
  這種藥物有副作用嗎？

already vs all ready

形近字詞分清楚

❓ 詞語辨析

already（單獨一字）是副詞，置於動詞 be 之後或一般動詞之前，意思是「已經；早已；曾經」。

all ready（分作二字）是形容詞片語，置於動詞 be 之後，意思是「完全準備好了」。

already 的發音是 /ɔːlˈred.i/，重音在第二個音節；all ready 則讀作 /ɔːlˈred.i/，分開兩個字讀出來。

⭐ 例句示範

already

- Dinner was **already** prepared when we got home.
  我們回到家時，晚餐已經準備好了。

- I asked him to go to the cinema but he'd **already** watched the film. 我約他去看電影，可他早就看過那套電影了。

all ready

- Are you **all ready**? Hurry up, we're late!
  你們都準備好了嗎？快點吧，我們遲到了！

- Everything is **all ready** for the party.
  一切都準備好了，派對可以隨時開始。

🔍 增潤知識

already 很多時候會用在完成式句子中，來表示某動作已經完成了一段時間。例如：

- I **have already returned** the books. 我已經還書了。

- The film **had already started** when we got to the cinema.
  我們到達電影院時，電影已經開始放映了。

angel vs angle

形近字詞分清楚

❓ 詞語辨析

angel（字尾是 -gel）作名詞用，意思是「天使」，也可用來比喻像天使般善良仁慈的人，或用來稱呼非常喜愛或熟悉的人。

angle（字尾是 -gle）也作名詞用，指「（兩條直線相交形成的）角」、「（建築物或家具等的）角；突出的部分」，以及「（思考問題的）角度；觀點」。

angel 發音為 /ˈeɪn.dʒəl/，angle 則為 /ˈæŋ.ɡəl/。

⭐ 例句示範

angel

- This artist likes to paint **angels**.
  這位畫家喜歡畫天使。

- Perry is no **angel**. He always fights with people.
  佩里不是善良的人，他經常和人打架。

- My little **angel**, it's time for bed. 小寶貝，是時候睡覺了。

angle

- Every square has four right **angles**. 所有正方形都有四個直角。

- I hit my foot against the **angle** of the coffee table and it hurts so much. 我的腳撞到了茶几的角，痛得要命。

🔍 增潤知識

短語 guardian angel 指「守護神；守護天使」。例如：

- Uncle Pang has been my **guardian angel**.
  彭叔叔一直是我的守護天使。

如指建築物或家具等的「角」或「突出的部分」，angle 可以由 corner 取代。

beside vs besides

形近字詞分清楚

❓ 詞語辨析

beside（字尾沒有 s）是介詞，指「在……旁邊」。

besides（字尾有 s）作介詞用時，指「除……之外，還有……」。它也可作副詞用，指「此外；而且」，用以提供另一個原因或事實來支持所説的話。

beside 讀作 /bɪˈsaɪd/，besides 則讀作 /bɪˈsaɪdz/。

⭐ 例句示範

beside

- Turn left and you'll see the cinema. It's **beside** a café.
  左轉就會看到電影院，它就在咖啡店旁邊。

besides

- What other sports do you like **besides** badminton?
  除了羽毛球外，你還喜歡其他運動嗎？

- I'm too tired to go out – **besides**, I have an exam tomorrow.
  我太累，不出去了──再說，我明天還要考試。

🔍 增潤知識

beside 是比較正式的説法，較為口語的説法是 next to。例如：

- Can I sit **next to** you? 我可以坐在你旁邊嗎？

相反，besides 則是口語上的説法，有時可用 what's more 來代替。而在書面語中，如作介詞用時，人們會用 except for 或 in addition to。作副詞用時，會用 moreover 或 in addition。例如：

- Everyone was there **except for** Tom.
  除了湯姆，大家都在那裏。

- The price is good and, **moreover**, the taste is great!
  價錢很不錯，還有味道非常好！

漫畫看一看

❓ 詞語辨析

breathe（拼寫結尾有 e）是動詞，指「呼吸」。

breath（拼寫結尾沒有 e）作不可數名詞用時，指「呼吸；氣息」；作可數名詞用時，指「一口氣」。

breathe 讀作 /briːð/，breath 則讀作 /breθ/。

★ 例句示範

breathe

- Fish **breathe** through their gills. 魚透過腮呼吸。

- She's **breathing** garlic fumes all over me!
  她口裏的大蒜味熏着我。

- Slowly **breathe** in and out. 緩緩吸氣呼氣。

breath

- Wait, I'm short of **breath**. 等一下，我上氣不接下氣。

- She took a deep **breath** and jumped into the water.
  她深呼吸一下，然後跳進水中。

🔍 增潤知識

動詞 breathe 也可指「小聲地說話」。例如：

- "I love you!" she **breathed** softly.
  「我愛你！」她溫柔地說。

有不少英文慣用語由 breath 組成。例如：

- **Hold your breath** for ten seconds. 屏住呼吸十秒。

- He arrived on the top floor **out of breath**.
  他氣喘吁吁地來到頂樓。

- She has **bad breath** today. 她今天有口氣。

❓ 詞語辨析

dairy（拼寫中間是 ai）作名詞時，解作「乳牛場」或「牛奶公司；乳品店」；作形容詞時，則解作「乳製品的；乳品的」。

diary（拼寫中間是 ia）是名詞，指「日記」或「日程簿」，複數是 diaries。

dairy 發音是 /ˈdeə.ri/，diary 則是 /ˈdaɪə.ri/。

⭐ 例句示範

dairy

- Dad buys milk at the **dairy** every morning.
  爸爸每天早上在乳品店買牛奶。

- **Dairy** products can provide us with enough protein.
  乳製品可以為我們提供足夠的蛋白質。

diary

- Have you kept a **diary**?
  你有寫日記嗎？

- Let's put the exam dates in the **diary**.
  我們把考試的日期寫在日程簿上吧。

🔍 增潤知識

dairy 作形容詞用時，必須放在名詞前。例如：dairy cattle（乳牛）、dairy farm（乳牛場）。

還有一個容易混淆的詞語是 daily，可作副詞或形容詞用，分別指「每天的」和「每天地」。例如：

- Take the medicine thrice **daily**.
  這藥每日服三次。

❓ 詞語辨析

desert（拼寫中間只有一個 s）作名詞用時，指「沙漠」。

dessert（拼寫中間有兩個 s）是名詞，指「甜品」。

desert 發音為 /ˈdez.ət/，重音在第一個音節；dessert 發音為 /dɪˈzɜːt/，重音在第二個音節。

⭐ 例句示範

desert

- The plane crashed in the **desert**. 飛機在沙漠上墜毀。

- The Sahara is the largest **desert** in the world.
  撒哈拉沙漠是世界上最大的沙漠。

dessert

- For **dessert** there's ice cream or pudding.
  甜品有雪糕和布丁可供選擇。

- My favourite **dessert** is apple pie.
  我最喜歡的甜品是蘋果批。

🔍 增潤知識

人們會用 desert 來比喻欠缺文化的地方。例如：

- This city is a cultural **desert**.
  這個城市是一片文化沙漠。

形容一個地方無人的、荒涼的，可以用形容詞 deserted。例如：

- At night the streets are **deserted**.
  晚上，街上空無一人。

desert 也可作動詞用，解作「拋棄；捨棄」。例如：

- He **deserted** his wife. 他拋棄了妻子。

envelop vs envelope

形近字詞分清楚

❓ 詞語辨析

envelop（拼寫結尾沒有 e）作動詞用，解作「包住；圍繞；籠罩」，過去式和過去分詞都是 enveloped。

envelope（拼寫結尾有 e）作名詞用，指「信封」。

envelop 發音是 /ɪnˈvel.əp/，重音在第二個音節；envelope 發音為 /ˈen.və.ləʊp/，重音在第一個音節。

⭐ 例句示範

envelop

- The mountain peaks are **enveloped** in mist.
  羣峰籠罩在薄霧中。

- That fragrant smell of flowers **enveloped** us.
  那股芬芳的花香籠罩着我們。

envelope

- Mum folded the letter and put it in an **envelope**.
  媽媽把信摺起，然後放入信封。

- He tore open the **envelope** to read the letter.
  他撕開信封，閱讀信件。

🔍 增潤知識

動詞 envelop 的用法比較正式，多見於文學作品。在一般場合或在口語中，人們會用上 cover 一詞。例如：

- Snow **covered** the hills.
  白雪覆蓋了山頭。

名詞 envelope 的複數是 envelopes，不是 envelops。

漫畫看一看

❓ 詞語辨析

everyday（單獨一字）作形容詞用，指「日常的；平常的」或「普通的」，用來表示經常發生的事情。

every day（分作二字）是描述時間頻率的片語，every 是 day 的形容詞，意思分別是「每一個」和「日子」，即是「每日」。

everyday 的發音是 /ˈev.ri.deɪ/，重音在第一個音節；every day 的發音是 /ˈev.ri deɪ/，分兩個字讀出。

★ 例句示範

everyday

- This novel describes the **everyday** lives of ordinary people.
  這部小說描述了老百姓的日常生活。

- We're just an **everyday** family, with a kid and bills to pay.
  我們只是一個普通家庭，有一個孩子，還有賬單要付。

every day

- Jonathan swims almost **every day**.
  喬納森幾乎每天都游泳。

- Dad worked **every day** last week – including Saturday and Sunday. 上個星期，爸爸每天都在工作，包括星期六和星期日。

🔍 增潤知識

我們可用以下的方法來判斷句子中應該使用 everyday 還是 every day。如果可以在 every 和 day 之間加入 single 這個字，而句子意思沒變，這表示必須使用分作二字的 every day。例如：

- I read **every (single) day**.
  我每天都閱讀。

漫畫看一看

This temple is one of the historic buildings of the city.

1910

It was built more than 100 years ago.

Was the statue a real historical figure?

Yes, he was. He was a general born around 1,000 years ago.

形近字詞分清楚

❓ 詞語辨析

historic（拼寫結尾沒有 al）作形容詞用，指「古老的；具有歷史意義的」，通常用來表示歷史上著名的、重要的事物。

historical（拼寫結尾有 al）作形容詞用，指「歷史上的；歷史學的」，通常用來指和歷史有關或是歷史上出現過的人或事。

historic 發音是 /hɪˈstɒr.ɪk/，historical 則是 /hɪˈstɒr.ɪ.kᵊl/。

⭐ 例句示範

historic

- There are many ancient **historic** sites around here.
  這裏附近有很多古老的歷史遺跡。

- The Blue House is one of the **historic** buildings in Hong Kong.
  藍屋是香港的歷史建築之一。

- "It is a **historic** moment," she told the press.
  「這是具有歷史意義的時刻。」她對記者說。

historical

- This is a **historical** novel.
  這是一部歷史小說。

- Was Qu Yuan a real **historical** figure?
  屈原是真實的歷史人物嗎？

- **Historical** research shows that Li Bai was born in Central Asia. 歷史研究指出李白生於中亞地區。

🔍 增潤知識

historic 和 historical 都是從名詞 history（歷史）衍生出來，所以兩者的意思都與歷史有關。

漫畫看一看

What's it?

It's a puppy. It's lovely, isn't it? Let's look after it.

Oh, I forgot to feed it. Where's its food?

It's been crying for a long time. What's wrong?

❓ 詞語辨析

it's（有撇號）是縮寫，它可以代表 it is 或 it has。it's 當作 it is 的用法最為常見，後面可接形容詞、名詞、動名詞等。如果是 it has 的縮寫，那便需要用完成式句型，即 has + 過去分詞。

its（沒有撇號）並不是縮寫，它只是 it 的所有格，代表「它的；牠的」，地位等同於 his、her、my、our、their 這些所有格代詞。

it's 和 its 都讀作 /ɪts/。

⭐ 例句示範

it's (= it is)

- **It's** a pop-up book. 它是一本立體書。
- **It's** very nice to meet you. 見到你真好。

it's (= it has)

- **It's** stopped raining. Let's go out for a walk.
  雨停了。我們出去散步吧。
- **It's** been a wonderful day. Thank you so much.
  這一天過得真愉快，太謝謝你了。

its

- He gave the puppy **its** food. 他給小狗食物。
- The tree has lost all of **its** leaves in winter.
  這棵樹在冬天掉光了葉子。

🔍 增潤知識

it's 不能當成 it was 的縮寫。be 的過去式 was 和 were 一般不可縮寫，因為縮寫的話會造成時態混淆。

漫畫看一看

❓ 詞語辨析

lately（字根是 late）作副詞用，意思是「最近；近來」。

lastly（字根是 last）作副詞用，意思是「最後」，常用於數說最後一個人或事。

lately 讀作 /ˈleɪt.li/，lastly 則讀作 /ˈlɑːst.li/。

⭐ 例句示範

lately

- Have you seen Peter **lately**? 你最近見過彼得嗎？

- Grandpa hasn't been too well **lately**. 爺爺最近身體不太好。

lastly

- **Lastly**, I'd like to thank everyone who has come to the party today. 最後，我想感謝每一位今天來參加派對的人。

- We need to buy cheese, milk, bread, and **lastly**, ice cream. 我們需要買芝士、牛奶、麵包，還有最後一樣，雪糕。

🔍 增潤知識

lately 與 recently 同義。例如：

- Have you seen any good films **lately / recently**? 你最近有看過什麼好電影嗎？

lastly 的反義詞是 firstly。例如：

- **Firstly**, let me thank everyone for coming here this evening. 首先，讓我感謝各位今晚的來臨。

lastly 由形容詞 last 加上詞尾 -ly 而成。last 指「最後的；最終的」。例如：

- I visited my grandparents **last** week. 我上星期探望過祖父母。

漫畫看一看

❓ 詞語辨析

later（拼寫中間只有一個 t）作副詞用時，指「晚些時候；過些時候」；作形容詞用時，指「晚一些；稍後的」。

latter（拼寫中間有兩個 t）作形容詞用時，指「後者的；後期的」；作名詞用時，則指「後者」。

later 發音為 /ˈleɪ.tər/，latter 則為 /ˈlæt.ə/。

⭐ 例句示範

later

- I'll be back **later**. Please wait for me.
  我稍後回來，請等等我。

- This old man lived alone in his **later** years.
  這位老人晚年獨居。

latter

- The **latter** part of the book is difficult to read.
  這本書的後半部很難讀。

- You can order ice cream or fruit tart, and the **latter** is delicious.
  你可以叫雪糕或水果撻，後者很好吃。

🔍 增潤知識

形容詞 later 的相反詞是 earlier。例如：

- The match should have set for an **earlier** date.
  比賽應該訂在早些的日期。

形容詞 latter 的相反詞則是 former。例如：the former headmaster（前任校長）、his former wife（他的前妻）。

latter 作名詞用時，必須與 the 連用，即 the latter。

漫畫看一看

It's too dark here. Is there any lighting in here?

Yes, but the electricity just went out.

Oh, we just can't see anything at all.

Unlike you, I can still find my way in darkness.

Now you can see under the flash of lightning.

形近字詞分清楚

❓ 詞語辨析

lighting（ing 前沒有 n）作名詞用，指「（房屋、劇院等處的）照明；燈光設計」。

lightning（ing 前有 n）作名詞用，指「閃電」。

lighting 發音是 /ˈlaɪ.tɪŋ/，lightning 則是 /ˈlaɪt.nɪŋ/。

⭐ 例句示範

lighting

- We need more **lighting** in the library.
  圖書館需要更多的照明設備。

- I prefer soft **lighting**.
  我比較喜歡柔和的燈光。

lightning

- The fisherman was struck by **lightning**.
  那個漁夫被閃電擊中了。

- What causes **lightning** and thunder?
  行雷閃電的成因為何？

🔍 增潤知識

lighting 是不可數名詞，沒有複數形式。

lightning 也是不可數名詞，沒有複數形式。如要表達數量，可加上量詞。例如：a flash / bolt of lightning（一道閃電）。

慣用語 like lightning 指「閃電般地；極快地」。例如：

- He moved over **like lightning** and caught the baby before she fell. 他眼明手快，一手抓住了嬰兒，沒有讓她摔倒。

漫畫看一看

❓詞語辨析

lose（拼寫中間只有一個 o）一般作及物動詞用，有多重意思，包括「遺失；失去；喪失；輸掉；減少」等，過去式和過去分詞都是 lost。

loose（拼寫中間有兩個 o）是形容詞，也有多個意思，包括「鬆的；鬆動的；鬆散的；寬鬆的；沒有束縛的」等。

lose 發音是 /luːz/，loose 則是 /luːs/。

⭐ 例句示範

lose

- I've **lost** my school bag.
  我弄丟了書包。

- Our team **lost** the basketball game.
  我們這隊輸了籃球比賽。

loose

- Your shoelaces are **loose**.
  你的鞋帶鬆了。

- My jeans become **loose** – I must have lost weight.
  我的牛仔褲變鬆了——我一定是瘦了。

🔍 增潤知識

動詞 lose 作「遺失」解時，相反詞是 find。例如：

- Have you **found** your wallet?
  你找到了錢包沒有？

動詞 lose 作「輸掉」解時，相反詞是 win。例如：

- Who **won** the race?
  誰贏了比賽？

形近字詞分清楚

❓ 詞語辨析

loss（拼寫結尾是 s）作名詞用，指「丟失；遺失；損失；虧損」。loss 的動詞是 lose（見第 20 課）。

lost（拼寫結尾是 t）是形容詞，指「迷路的；走失的；丟失的；失蹤的；迷惘的」等。lost 是動詞 lose 的過去式和過去分詞（見第 20 課）。

loss 發音 /lɒs/，lost 則是 /lɒst/。

⭐ 例句示範

loss

- He felt a sense of **loss** when he studied abroad alone.
  他獨自在外國讀書時，感到一絲失落感。

- The company made a big **loss** last year.
  公司去年錄得嚴重虧損。

lost

- The police found the **lost** child near the lake.
  警方在湖邊找到了那名失蹤的兒童。

- "Do you understand?" "Not really. I'm a bit **lost**."
  「你懂我的意思嗎？」「不太明白，我有點迷惘。」

🔍 增潤知識

慣用語 be at a loss 指「困惑；不知所措」。例如：

- He felt completely **at a loss** when he got lost.
  他迷路了，完全不知所措。

慣用語 be lost in thought 指「陷入沉思」。例如：

- Sandy just sat there, **lost in thought**.
  桑迪就坐在那裏，陷入沉思。

漫畫看一看

形近字詞分清楚

❓ 詞語辨析

medal（拼寫中間是 d）作可數名詞用時，指「獎章；獎牌；勳章；紀念章」；作不及物動詞用時，指「（在體育比賽中）獲得獎牌」。

metal（拼寫中間是 t）作名詞用，指「金屬」。

medal 讀作 /ˈmed.ᵊl/，metal 則讀作 /ˈmet.ᵊl/。

⭐ 例句示範

medal

- She won a gold **medal** at the Olympics.
  她在奧林匹克運動會上贏得一枚金牌。

- Hong Kong has the potential to **medal** in swimming this year.
  香港今年有可能在游泳比賽上贏得獎牌。

metal

- This door is made of **metal**.
  這扇門是用金屬造的。

- Gold and silver are precious **metals**.
  金和銀都是貴金屬。

🔍 增潤知識

常與 medal 搭配的動詞除了 win 之外，還有 award 和 compete for。例如：

- Two girls were **awarded medals** for their bravey.
  兩名女孩因英勇表現而獲得勳章。

- The swimmers are **competing for** the gold **medal**.
  這些泳手在爭奪金牌。

漫畫看一看

形近字詞分清楚

❓ 詞語辨析

open（字尾沒有 ed）作形容詞用時，有多種意思，例如「（盒子、窗戶等）開着的」或「（商店、圖書館等）開放的；正在營業的」。

opened（字尾有 ed）是動詞 open 的過去式，其中一個意思是「開門；開始營業」。

open 發音是 /ˈəʊ.pən/，opened 則是 /ˈəʊ.pənd/。

⭐ 例句示範

open

- Someone has left the windows **open**. 有人把窗戶敞開着。

- The baby is not asleep; his eyes are **open**.
  寶寶還未睡着，眼睛還睜開着。

- Is the library **open** yet? 圖書館開門了嗎？

open(ed)

- The museum **opens** at ten o'clock. 博物館十點開門。

- This supermarket **opened** last year. 這間超市去年開始營業。

- The new shop will be officially **opened** by the chairman next week. 這間新商店下周將由主席正式宣佈開業。

🔍 增潤知識

雖然 open 可用作動詞，但是不能用於被動語態，因為它是個瞬間動詞（instant verb），即是動作在一瞬間發生和結束，動作結束之後就以「狀態」的形式存在。例如，當門窗被打開後，就維持「開着」的狀態。因此，我們不能說：The window was opened. 而說：The window was open.（那扇窗是開着的。）

形近字詞分清楚

❓ 詞語辨析

past（拼寫結尾是 t）是「過去」的意思，用在時間或空間上，可以是形容詞、名詞或副詞。

pass（拼寫結尾是 s）可以是動詞，意思很多，例如「通過（考試）」、「經過；路過」或「傳遞（東西）」等，過去式與過去分詞是 passed。pass 也可以是名詞，指「入場券」。

past 讀作 /pɑːst/，pass 則讀作 /pɑːs/。

⭐ 例句示範

past

- I haven't seen Tom for the **past** few days.
  我這幾天都沒有見到湯姆。

- The car drove **past** me at high speed.
  那輛車以高速在我身邊駛過。

- In the **past**, people wrote on bamboo.
  以前，人們在竹枝上寫字。

pass

- Did he **pass** the driving test? 他通過駕駛考試嗎？

- **Pass** the salt, please. 請把鹽遞過來。

- Can you show your boarding **pass**? 可以看一下你的登機證嗎？

🔍 增潤知識

不要把 pass 或 passed 寫成 past，因為 past 不能當動詞用。例如我們不能説：I past her in the corridor this morning. 而説：I passed her in the corridor this morning.（今天早上我在走廊與她擦肩而過。）

漫畫看一看

❓ 詞語辨析

patience（拼寫結尾是 ce）是不可數名詞，也是抽象名詞，指「忍耐；耐心」。

patients（拼寫結尾是 ts）是名詞 patient（病人）的複數。patient 一字也可作形容詞用，指「有耐心的；忍耐的」。

patience 發音是 /ˈpeɪ.ʃ°ns/，patients 則是 /ˈpeɪ.ʃ°ntz/。

⭐ 例句示範

patience

- The shopkeeper lost his **patience** and shouted at me.
  那店主失去了耐性，對我大呼大叫起來。

patient

- There are 300 **patients** in this hospital.
  這間醫院有 300 個病人。

- I know you're hungry; just be **patient** and dinner will be ready soon. 我知道你肚子餓，還是忍耐一下吧，晚餐快準備好了。

🔍 增潤知識

patience 沒有複數形式，不能說 patiences。如果想要表達很有耐性，可以用量詞 a lot of。例如：

- You need **a lot of patience** to be a nurse.
  當護士要很有耐性。

形容詞 patient 的相反詞是 impatient。例如：

- John's trouble is that he's too **impatient**.
  約翰的缺點是沒有耐心。

漫畫看一看

I won the first prize in the talent show!

Congratulations!

I can sell this golden cup for you for a very good price!

Forget it! It brings shame on me if I sell it for money!

❓ 詞語辨析

price（拼寫中間是 c）作名詞用，指「價格；價錢」。

prize（拼寫中間是 z）作名詞用，指「獎；獎賞」，例如因贏得比賽或工作表現優秀而獲得的獎金或獎品。

price 讀作 /praɪs/，prize 讀作 /praɪz/，兩字的讀音十分接近，差別在於尾音。

⭐ 例句示範

price

- What's the **price**? 價錢多少？
- The **prices** keep going up. 價格持續上升。
- I bought these T-shirts at half **price** in the sale.
  我在特價時以半價買了這些短袖汗衫。

prize

- He won the second **prize** in the competition.
  他在比賽中獲得亞軍。
- His novel has won several literary **prizes**.
  他的小說獲得多個文學獎。

🔍 增潤知識

price 可用來指「代價」。例如：

- He has to study on most weekends, but that's the **price** of success. 他大部分周末都得要溫習，但那就是成功的代價。

prize 可用來指「難能可貴的東西」。例如：

- The **prize** would be fame. 最理想是得到榮譽。

quiet vs quite

漫畫看一看

形近字詞分清楚

❓ 詞語辨析

quiet（拼寫結尾是 iet）一般作形容詞用，意思是「安靜的；寧靜的」。

quite（拼寫結尾是 ite）是程度副詞，表示「很；頗為；相當」。

quiet 發音 /ˈkwaɪ.ət/，有兩個音節；quite 發音 /kwaɪt/，只有一個音節。

⭐ 例句示範

quiet

- We'll have to be **quiet** so as not to wake grandma.
  我們得安靜點，免得吵醒祖母。

- It was midnight and the streets were **quiet**.
  午夜時分，街上一片靜寂。

quite

- The film was **quite** good, but the novel was much better.
  電影還不錯，但小說更好看。

- She has got **quite** a lot of friends. 她有很多朋友。

🔍 增潤知識

人們在口語中會説 Quiet!、Be quiet! 或 Keep quiet!，來示意別人安靜點。例如：

- **Be quiet!** I'm on the phone. 安靜點！我正在通電話。

英語有多個表示「很；相當」的程度副詞，按語氣輕重程度排列，分別是 fairly（還算）、quite（很）、rather / pretty（相當）、very（十分），當中以 very 的語氣最強。例如：

- This book is **fairly / quite / pretty / very** interesting.
  這本書還算 / 很 / 相當 / 十分有趣。

漫畫看一看

By the time I got to the finish line, I was covered in sweet!

Why? Did people throw sweets at you?

No. It's because it's very hot indeed.

You're saying you were covered in sweat, right?

Oh, yes.

形近字詞分清楚 ✏️

❓ 詞語辨析

sweat（拼寫中間是 ea）是名詞，解作「汗水」；亦是不及物動詞，解作「流汗」，後面無需接賓語。

sweet（拼寫中間是 ee）作形容詞用時，有多重意義，可指「（食物或飲料）甜的」、「（人或物）討人喜歡的」、「（聲音）悅耳的」或「（氣味）芬芳的」；作名詞用時指「糖果」，即美式英語中的 candy。

sweat 讀作 /swet/，sweet 則讀作 /swi:t/。

⭐ 例句示範

sweat

- **Sweat** poured down her face. 她汗流滿面。

- It was so hot and we all started to **sweat**.
  天氣太熱，我們所有人都開始流汗。

sweet

- The pear is **sweet** and juicy. 這個梨又甜又多汁。

- What a **sweet** voice you have! 你的聲音多甜美！

- How **sweet** of you to remember my birthday!
  你真好，記得我的生日！

🔍 增潤知識

名詞 sweat 是不可數的，沒有複數形式，不能説 a sweat 或 a lot of sweats。

在英式英語中，sweet 與 dessert 同義，指餐後的甜品。例如：

- I'm full, I really couldn't manage a **sweet**.
  我吃飽了，真的吃不下甜品了。

thorough vs through

漫畫看一看

❓ 詞語辨析

thorough（拼寫中間有兩個 o）作形容詞用，解作「仔細的；完全的；徹底的」。

through（拼寫中間只有一個 o）多作介詞用，指「（空間）從一邊去到另一邊」，即是「通過；穿越」，也指「（時間）由始至終；從頭到尾」。

thorough 發音是 /ˈθʌr.ə/，through 則是 /θruː/。

⭐ 例句示範

thorough

- The doctor gave us a **thorough** check-up.
  醫生給我們做了全面的身體檢查。

- The police investigation was very **thorough**.
  警方的調查十分徹底。

through

- We walked **through** the carpark to the shopping mall.
  我們穿過停車場，來到購物商場。

- She screamed when the rollercoaster went **through** a dark tunnel. 過山車穿越黑暗的隧道時，她尖叫起來。

🔍 增潤知識

thorough 的副詞是 thoroughly，解作「非常；徹底地」。例如：

- I **thoroughly** enjoyed the show. 我非常喜歡這個演出。

through 也作形容詞用，指「（火車、巴士等）直達的；中途不停站的」。例如：

- We took a **through** bus to Guangzhou.
  我們乘坐直通巴士去廣州。

漫畫看一看

❓ 詞語辨析

though（拼寫中間有 h）是連接詞，與 although 同義，解作「雖然；儘管」或「可是；不過」。

tough（拼寫中間沒有 h）是形容詞，包含多重意義，例如「（事物）結實的；堅硬的；嚴厲的；困難的」或「（人）堅強的」等。

though 發音 /ðəʊ/，tough 則是 /tʌf/。

⭐ 例句示範

though

• **Though** he was poor, he was happy. 他雖然窮，但他很快樂。

• They will throw a party, **though** I don't know which day.
他們要開派對，但我不知道是哪天。

tough

• This meat is **tough**. 這塊肉很不好嚼。

• The exam was so **tough** that only one student passed.
考試太難了，只有一個學生及格。

• People think Katy is **tough**, but she's easily frightened.
別人以為凱蒂很堅強，但其實她很容易受驚嚇。

🔍 增潤知識

though 前面加上 even，可讓詞義更加強烈。例如：

• **Even though** he was ill, he still managed to win the competition. 儘管他生病了，但他最終還是贏出了比賽。

此外，不要混淆 though 和 thought。thought 是動詞 think（思考）的過去式和過去分詞，也可作名詞用，指「思想」。

形近字詞分清楚

❓ 詞語辨析

on TV（拼寫中間沒有 the）指「出現在電視熒幕上」。這裏的 TV 指電視節目，是抽象的東西。

on the TV（拼寫中間有 the）指「在電視機上」或「在電視機上方」。這裏的 TV 指電視機，是實實在在的東西。

⭐ 例句示範

on TV

- Look! Dad is **on TV** now. 看！爸爸上電視了。

- What's **on TV** now – anything special?
  現在有什麼電視節目——有什麼好看的嗎？

- The children love to watch cartoons **on TV**.
  孩子喜歡看電視上的卡通片。

on the TV

- My cat always sleeps **on the TV**.
  我的貓兒常常在電視機上面睡覺。

- Don't put anything **on the TV**.
  不要在電視機上放東西。

- The remote is out of order. Is there any button **on the TV**?
  遙控壞了，電視機上有按鈕嗎？

🔍 增潤知識

TV 是縮寫詞，全寫是 television，俗語叫 telly 或 the box。例如：

- What's on **telly** tonight? 今晚有什麼電視節目？

- There's nothing worth watching on **the box**.
  電視沒有什麼值得一看。

形近字詞分清楚

❓ 詞語辨析

wander（拼寫中間是 a）作動詞用，指「遊蕩；閒逛」。

wonder（拼寫中間是 o）作不及物動詞用時，解作「疑惑；想知道」或「感到吃驚」。

wander 發音是 /ˈwɒn.dər/，wonder 則是 /ˈwʌn.dər/。

⭐ 例句示範

wander

- They were just **wandering** the streets, doing nothing.
  他們只是百無聊賴地在街上徘徊。

- Don't **wander** off! 別走遠！

wonder

- I **wonder** why David is always late for school.
  我奇怪大衞為什麼上學老是遲到。

- We all **wondered** at her rudeness.
  我們都對她的無禮感到吃驚。

🔍 增潤知識

wander 與 mind 連用時，解作「心不在焉」或「（因年老而）神志恍惚」。例如：

- My mind started to **wander**.
  我開始心不在焉了。

wonder 也可作名詞用，解作「驚歎」或「奇觀」。例如：

- They were filled with **wonder** when they saw the waterfall.
  他們看到瀑布時驚歎不已。

漫畫看一看

The rabbit family has been living on the isle for many years.

Aisle? They must be very poor! Why don't they seek help?

No! They're not poor. In fact, they're very rich. They live on an island owned by them.

Oh, you're talking about the isle on which they live!

同音字詞分清楚

❓ 詞語辨析

aisle（開首是 a）是名詞，意思是「通道；過道」，例如飛機上供乘客行走的走道，或電影院和教堂座席間的走道，也指商店裏貨架間的通道。

isle（開首沒有 a）是名詞，意思是「島」，與 island 同義，多數用於地名。

aisle 和 isle 發音相同，都是 /aɪl/，兩者中間的 s 都不發音。

⭐ 例句示範

aisle

- We followed the usher down the **aisle**.
  我們跟着領座員沿着通道走過去。

- You'll find the biscuits in the third **aisle** from the entrance.
  你可在入口處數起第三個通道找到餅乾。

isle

- Can you find the British **Isles** on the map?
  你能在地圖上找到不列顛羣島嗎？

- Have you ever been to the **Isle** of Man? 你有去過曼島嗎？

🔍 增潤知識

aisle 和 isle 都是可數名詞。前者的複數是 aisles；後者則是 isles。

英文俗語 go / walk down the aisle，指一對新人步入教堂的紅毯走道，即「結婚」之意。例如：

- She's the youngest, but she's the first one who **went / walked down the aisle**. 她年紀最輕，卻最早結婚。

漫畫看一看

同音字詞分清楚 🖉

❓ 詞語辨析

brake（拼寫結尾是 ake）作名詞用時，解作「剎車掣」；作動詞用時，則指「剎停；迅速停下」。

break（拼寫結尾是 eak）作名詞用時，解作「短暫的休息；假期」；作及物動詞用時，指「打破；弄壞（某物）」等；作不及物動詞用時，則指「破碎；破裂」。

brake 和 brake 發音相同，都讀作 /breɪk/。

⭐ 例句示範

brake

- This bicycle has no **brakes**. It's not safe.
  這輛單車沒有剎車掣，這樣不安全。

- Don't drive too fast, or you cannot **brake** easily.
  不要開得太快，否則不容易剎車。

break

- Let's have a tea **break** now. 我們喝杯茶休息一下吧。

- They'll fly to Shanghai during the Christmas **break**.
  他們會在聖誕假期飛去上海。

- The boys **broke** the window with their football.
  那些男孩踢球打碎了玻璃窗。

- The vase fell to the floor and **broke**. 花瓶掉到地上摔碎了。

🔍 增潤知識

慣用語 put the brakes on 是個比喻，意思是「控制；制止」。例如：

- We have to **put the brakes on** this project.
  我們不得不終止這個項目。

❓ 詞語辨析

die（拼寫中間是 i）是不及物動詞，解作「死亡」，過去式和過去分詞是 died，現在分詞是 dying。

dye（拼寫中間是 y）作及物動詞用時，解作「給……染色」，過去式和過去分詞是 dyed，現在分詞是 dyeing。

die 和 dye 的發音相同，都讀作 /daɪ/。

⭐ 例句示範

die

- She **died** peacefully in her sleep. 她在睡夢中安然辭世。
- Many people have a fear of **dying**. 很多人害怕死亡。

dye

- Lily **dyed** her hair pink. 莉莉把頭髮染成粉紅色。
- The children are **dyeing** their own T-shirts.
  那些孩子正在為自己的短袖汗衫染色。

🔍 增潤知識

die 的名詞是 death，指「死亡」；dye 的名詞同樣是 dye，指「染料」。

die 可用來比喻電器因沒電而停止運轉。例如：

- I'm sorry I didn't answer your call – my cellphone **died**.
  對不起，我沒有接你電話──我的手機沒電了。

俗語 be dying for something 指「渴望得到某東西」。例如：

- He **is dying for** a cup of coffee.
  他很想喝咖啡。

漫畫看一看

❓ 詞語辨析

flea（拼寫結尾是 ea）是名詞，意思是「蚤；跳蚤」，複數是 fleas。

flee（拼寫結尾是 ee）是動詞，指「（因危險或恐懼而）逃走；逃跑」，可及物或不及物。過去式和過去分詞是 fled，現在分詞是 fleeing。

flea 和 flee 發音相同，都是 /fliː/。

⭐ 例句示範

flea

- This stray dog has **fleas**. 這隻流浪狗身上有跳蚤。

- He found a **flea** in his hair. 他在頭髮裏找到了一隻蚤。

flee

- They turned and **fled** when they heard the scream.
  他們聽到尖叫聲，就轉身逃跑。

- Many people **fled** the city during the war.
  戰爭期間很多人逃出了這個城市。

- Refugees began to **flee** to a neighbouring country.
  難民開始逃到鄰國去。

🔍 增潤知識

flee 是比較書面的說法。在日常生活中，人們一般會用 escape 或更口語化的 get away。例如：

- The thief **escaped** through the window.
  盜賊穿過一扇窗戶逃走了。

- Don't let him **get away**! 別讓他逃跑！

漫畫看一看

Now the war is over. May there be peace in the world.

The two countries have already agreed to a peace talk.

That's a good piece of news!

But rest in peace for those who died in the war.

❓ 詞語辨析

peace（拼寫中間是 ea）作不可數名詞用，指「和平；太平」，也指「安靜；寧靜」。

piece（拼寫中間是 ie）作可數名詞用，指「一塊；一片；一張」或「碎片」。

peace 和 piece 發音相同，都讀作 /piːs/。

⭐ 例句示範

peace

- All of us wish for world **peace**. 我們所有人都希望世界和平。

- I don't want to talk now. Just leave me in **peace**.
  我現在不想說話，讓我靜一下吧。

piece

- She torn off a **piece** of cloth from her dress.
  她從裙子撕下一塊布來。

- Jessie cut the pizza into eight **pieces**. 潔西把薄餅切成八塊。

🔍 增潤知識

慣用語 at peace 指「長眠；安息」。例如：

- Now the old man is **at peace** and his suffering is over.
  現在老人安息了，痛苦也結束了。

墓碑銘文上經常看到 RIP 三個字母，全寫是 rest in peace，解作「願靈魂安息」。

piece 是量詞，用途十分廣泛，可以與不可數名詞搭配以表示數量。例如：a piece of bread（一片麵包）/ a piece of paper（一張紙）/ a piece of wood（一塊木頭）等。

漫畫看一看

The hawk is hunting for its prey.

The lion is chasing its prey, too.

We have to love each other. We shall not kill.

Let's pray for peace on the grassland.

同音字詞分清楚

❓ 詞語辨析

pray（拼寫中間是 a）作不及物動詞用，意思是「祈禱；禱告」，也指「懇求；祈望」。

prey（拼寫中間是 e）作動詞用時，指「捕獵」；作名詞用時，則指「獵物」。

pray 和 prey 的發音相同，同為 /preɪ/。

⭐ 例句示範

pray

- They **prayed** silently inside a church.
  他們在教堂裏默默禱告。

- We're **praying** for good weather tomorrow.
  我們期盼明天會有好天氣。

- The blind man **prayed** that his sight might be restored.
  那個盲人祈望自己的視力能夠恢復。

prey

- Cats **prey** on mice and birds.
  貓捕食老鼠和雀鳥。

- The tiger has been stalking its **prey** for half an hour.
  老虎跟蹤牠的獵物半個小時了。

🔍 增潤知識

prey 是不可數名詞，沒有複數形式。例如我們不說：These frogs are easy preys for eagles. 而說：These frogs are easy prey for eagles.（這些青蛙容易成為老鷹的獵物。）

principal vs principle

As a principal, I won't allow any bullying in this school.

It's against the school principles and should never be tolerated.

From today, our teachers will teach you a set of principles.

The principal reason is for you to know what's right and what's wrong.

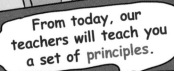

❓ 詞語辨析

principal（拼寫結尾是 pal）作名詞用時，指「校長」；作形容詞用時，指「主要的；最重要的」。

principle（拼寫結尾是 ple）作名詞用，指「原理；原則」或「道德原則；（行為）準則」。

principal 和 principle 發音相同，都讀作 /ˈprɪn.sə.pᵊl/。

⭐ 例句示範

principal

- This is just a small school with five teachers and a **principal**.
  這是一間小學校，只有五名教師和一名校長。

- What is your **principal** reason for taking singing lessons?
  你上唱歌班的主要原因是什麼？

- The **principal** character in the story is a mermaid.
  這個故事的主角是一條美人魚。

principle

- The basic **principle** is that all children have the right to
  education. 基本原則是所有兒童都有接受教育的權利。

- It's against my **principles** to tell lies. 說謊有違我的原則。

🔍 增潤知識

在美式英語，principal 指中小學的校長。但在英式英語，principal 指大學或學院的校長；中小學的校長一般叫 headteacher。

慣用語 in principle 指「原則上；基本上」。例如：

- They have accepted our proposal **in principle**.
  他們基本上已經接受了我們的建議書。

stationary vs stationery

❓ 詞語辨析

stationary（拼寫中間是 a）作形容詞用，形容事物或狀態「不動的；固定的；穩定的；不變的」。

stationery（拼寫中間是 e）作名詞用，指「文具」。

stationary 和 stationery 發音相同，同樣讀 /ˈsteɪ.ʃən.ᵊr.i/。

⭐ 例句示範

stationary

- Nobody is swimming. The water in the pool is **stationary**.
  沒有人在游泳，池水是靜止的。

- **Stationary** cars in traffic jams worsen the problem of air pollution. 交通堵塞，車輛停住不動，加劇了空氣污染問題。

stationery

- What **stationery** do we need for school?
  我們上學需要什麼文具？

- Is there any **stationery** store nearby? 附近有文具店嗎？

🔍 增潤知識

stationery 是文具的總稱，是不可數名詞，沒有複數形式。例如我們不能說：This shop sells stationeries. 而說：This shop sells stationery.（這商店出售文具。）

stationery 還有一個意思，指「（酒店房間提供的）優質信紙、信封」。例如：

- As people stopped writing in letters, hotel **stationery** began to disappear. 隨着人們不再寫信，酒店的信紙、信封逐漸消失了。

waist vs waste

同音字詞分清楚

❓ 詞語辨析

waist（拼寫中間有 i）作名詞用，指「腰；腰部」。

waste（拼寫中間沒有 i，結尾加 e）解作「浪費」，作單數或不可數名詞用，也作及物動詞用。

waist 和 waste 發音相同，都是 /weɪst/。

⭐ 例句示範

waist

- Lily wore a belt around her **waist**.
  莉莉在腰上束了一條腰帶。

- Use a tape to measure your **waist**.
  用卷尺來量度你的腰圍。

waste

- The meeting is a complete **waste** of time.
  那個會議簡直就是浪費時間。

- Don't **waste** food – eat everything on your plate.
  不要浪費食物，把碟子上所有東西都吃光。

- We **wasted** no time getting our prizes.
  我們第一時間就去拿獎品。

🔍 增潤知識

waste 也可解作「垃圾；廢料；廢物」，作不可數名詞用。例如：industrial waste（工業廢料）、human waste（人類排泄物）。又例如：

- Millions tons of **household waste** are produced each year.
  每年有數以百萬噸的家居垃圾產生。

weather vs whether

同音字詞分清楚 ✏️

❓ 詞語辨析

weather（拼寫中間是 ea）作不可數名詞用，指「天氣」。

whether（拼寫中間是 he）作連接詞用，解作「是否」，特別用於轉述問題或表達疑問，很多時與 or not 連用。

weather 和 whether 發音相同，讀作 /ˈweð.əʳ/，重音都在第一個音節。

⭐ 例句示範

weather

- The **weather** is lovely today. 今天的天氣真好。
- The match was cancelled due to the bad **weather**.
  受惡劣天氣影響，球賽取消了。

whether

- She asked him **whether** he'd mind if she opened the window.
  她問他是否介意她打開窗子。
- I'm not sure **whether** Johnny is at home. 我不肯定強尼是否在家。
- He can't decide **whether** to go **or not**. 他決定不了去還是不去。

🔍 增潤知識

weather 也可作動詞用，指「受到風雨侵蝕」。例如：

- The paint on the fences has **weathered** badly.
  籬笆上的油漆風吹日曬，褪色得很厲害。

我們用 whether...or...（不管……還是……）來引出兩種或多種可能性。例如：

- Someone has to tell mum, **whether** it's you **or** me.
  總得有人告訴媽媽，不論是你還是我。

alone vs lonely

❓ 詞語辨析

alone 作形容詞或副詞用，分別指「單獨的」和「獨自地」，強調獨自一人，但沒有感到孤獨。

lonely 作形容詞用，指「孤單的；寂寞的」，強調因為沒有人在身邊而感到孤獨。

⭐ 例句示範

alone

- I like to be **alone**. 我喜歡獨來獨往。

- She lives all **alone** but she never feels lonely.
  她獨居，但從未感到孤單。

lonely

- Lily feels very **lonely** without her parents.
  父母不在，莉莉感到非常寂寞。

- I get so **lonely** here with no one to talk to.
  在這裏沒人跟我說話，我感到非常孤獨。

🔍 增潤知識

慣用語 leave me alone 的字面意思是「留下我一個人」，但實際表達的意思是「讓我一個人靜一靜」或「請別打擾我」。例如：

- **Leave me alone!** I don't want to see you anymore!
  讓我靜一靜！我不想再見到你！

lonely 不作副詞用，例如我們不説：He is afraid to travel lonely. 而説：He is afraid to travel alone.（他害怕獨自旅行。）

lonely 的名詞是 loneliness，指「孤獨；寂寞」。例如：

- She has a fear of **loneliness**. 她害怕孤獨。

漫畫看一看

意近字詞分清楚

❓ 詞語辨析

among 作介詞用，指「在……之中」或「為……所環繞」，特別指在三個或以上的人或物之中。

between 也作介詞用，指「在（兩者）之間」，可指時間上、空間上或數量上。

⭐ 例句示範

among

- We found a gold coin **among** the bushes.
  我們在灌木叢中發現了一枚金幣。

- He divided the cake **among** the children.
  他把蛋糕分給了小孩。

- It's nice to be **among** friends. 和朋友在一起，感覺真好。

between

- The shop is open **between** 10 a.m. and 8 p.m.
  這間商店的營業時間為上午 10 時至晚上 8 時。

- There is a wall **between** the two houses.
  兩所房子之間有一道牆。

- These children are aged **between** 8 and 12.
  這些兒童年齡介乎 8 至 12 歲。

🔍 增潤知識

among 也可作 amongst，兩者意思和用法一樣。

between 只能用於兩個人或物（即兩個名詞）之間。兩者之間用 and 來連接。例如：

- Lucy sits **between** Peter **and** Jack. 露西坐在彼得和傑克之間。

bored vs boring

意近字詞分清楚

❓ 詞語辨析

bored（字尾是 -ed）是形容詞，用來形容人，指「感到無聊；感到厭煩」。

boring（字尾是 -ing）也是形容詞，用來形容事物，指「無聊的；乏味的」。

⭐ 例句示範

bored

- It was a rainy day and the children were **bored**.
  那是一個下雨天，孩子們都感到很無聊。

- Lily grew **bored** with her job. 莉莉開始對自己的工作感到厭煩。

boring

- The film was so **boring** that we all fell asleep.
  這部電影非常無聊，我們都睡着了。

- Benny finds the talk **boring**. 班尼覺得那場講座很乏味。

🔍 增潤知識

英語有很多詞根相同，但詞尾結構不同的形容詞。在這些形容詞中，以 -ed 結尾的字詞，用來表達人的感受；以 -ing 結尾的字詞，則描述事情令人感到某種感受。這個規律適用於許多形容詞：

形容人		形容事物	
excited	興奮的	**exciting**	令人興奮的
relaxed	放鬆的	**relaxing**	令人放鬆的
surprised	驚訝的	**surprising**	讓人驚訝的

意近字詞分清楚

❓ 詞語辨析

borrow 一般作及物動詞用,指「借入」,即是向別人借東西,句型是 to borrow something from someone。

lend 一般也是作及物動詞用,指「借出」,即是把東西借給別人,句型是 to lend something (to someone),過去式和過去分詞都是 lent。

⭐ 例句示範

borrow

- Could I **borrow** your suitcase, please?
  請問我可以借用你的行李箱嗎?

- Let's **borrow** that book **from** the library.
  我們去圖書館把那本書借回來吧。

lend

- I never **lend** my bicycle **to** anyone.
  我從來都不會借出我的單車。

- Can you **lend** me that book for a few days?
  你可以把那本書借給我看幾天嗎?

🔍 增潤知識

borrow 和 lend 在字面上都解作「借」,所以容易讓人混淆,例如當我們向別人借東西,我們要麼說:Can I borrow your dictionary?(我可以借用你的字典嗎?)或 Can you lend me your dictionary?(你可以把字典借給我嗎?)但千萬別說:Can I lend your dictionary? 或 Can you borrow me your dictionary?

❓ 詞語辨析

bring 作及物動詞用，指「帶來；拿來」，即是把某人或物從別處帶來或拿來。過去式和過去分詞是 brought。

take 作及物動詞用，指「帶去；拿走」，即是把某人或物帶走或拿走到別處。過去式是 took，過去分詞是 taken。

⭐ 例句示範

bring

- Can I **bring** my friend to the party?
  我可以帶朋友來參加派對嗎？

- You can take that book home, but **bring** it back on Friday.
  你可以把那本書帶回家，不過星期五要帶回來。

take

- Can you **take** this book to the library, please?
  請問你可以把這本書拿去圖書館嗎？

- Who has **taken** my dictionary? 誰拿走了我的字典？

🔍 增潤知識

如果在 bring 和 take 後面加 out，即 bring out 和 take out，兩者意思相同，都表示「拿出來」。例如：

- Ruby **brought out** / **took out** her books from her schoolbag.
  露比從書包拿出書本。

另一個和 bring 容易混淆的動詞是 fetch。bring 指「把某物帶到別處」，fetch 則是指「去別處取某物」。例如：

- Can you **fetch** me some bread when you go to the shop?
  你去商店時，能給我帶些麵包回來嗎？

意近字詞分清楚

❓ 詞語辨析

empathy（字首是 em-）作名詞用，解作「同理心；同感；共鳴」。

sympathy（字首是 sym-）作名詞用，解作「同情心」。

⭐ 例句示範

empathy

- She has great **empathy** with animals. 她對動物充滿同理心。

- Do you know what they've been through? You simply have no **empathy** for anybody!
你知道他們所經歷的一切嗎？你可沒有半點同理心呢！

sympathy

- They have a lot of **sympathy** for the orphans.
他們非常同情那些孤兒。

- I have no **sympathy** for them. It's their own fault.
我並不同情他們，這是他們自己的錯。

🔍 增潤知識

empathy 和 sympathy 的字根都是 -pathy，意思是「感覺」。

empathy 的字首 em- 有「在裏面」的意思，就像理解對方心頭裏的感受；sympathy 的字首 sym- 指「在旁邊」，可以理解成從旁同情對方。

empathy 只能作不可數名詞用，沒有複數形式。

sympathy 一般作不可數名詞用，偶然也會作複數名詞用，解作「支持」。例如：

- Their **sympathies** lie firmly with the government.
他們堅決支持政府。

farther vs further

漫畫看一看

How much farther is it to the peak?

It's about one more hour's walk.

I'm afraid I can't go any further. I feel so tired.

Come on! Let's take a break first. We have to get to the peak before dark.

❓ 詞語辨析

farther（拼寫中間是 a）作副詞用，指「更遠；較遠」，多用於表示實際的距離。

further（拼寫中間是 u）也作副詞用，同樣指「更遠；較遠」，但除了表示空間上的實際距離外，還指程度上的更進一步。

⭐ 例句示範

farther

- They live in the **farther** side of town.
  他們住在城裏較遠的地方。

- Can you stand a little **farther** away?
  你可以稍微站遠一點嗎？

further

- We can't go any **further**; it's too dark.
  我們沒辦法再走了，天很黑了。

- The police decided to investigate **further**.
  警方決定作出進一步調查。

🔍 增潤知識

表示空間上的距離時，farther 和 further 是同義詞。而在日常英語中，人們一般用 further，不用 farther。

farther 也可作形容詞用，解作「更遠的」。例如：

- A big tree stands at the **farther** end of the park.
  公園的那一頭有一棵大樹。

further 同樣也可作形容詞用，解作「更多的；額外的」。例如：

- Are there any **further** questions? 還有其他問題嗎？

漫畫看一看

Anything wrong with my report, doc?

You've put on a lot of weight. Why's that?

Well, I eat a lot more than before but go to the gym fewer times a week.

You ought to exercise more and eat less.

Okay.

❓ 詞語辨析

fewer 是 few 的比較級形容詞，表示數量上「較少的；少一些的」，與可數名詞連用。

less 是 little 的比較級形容詞，也是表示數量上「較少的」，與不可數名詞連用。

⭐ 例句示範

fewer

- **Fewer** and **fewer** pandas are left in the wild today.
  如今野生大熊貓的數量越來越少。

- I have **fewer** comic books than he does. 我的漫畫書比他少。

less

- You ought to eat **less** sugar. 你應該吃少一點糖分。

- We now do **less** homework than we did before.
  我們現在做的功課比以前少。

🔍 增潤知識

人們在口語中或會用 less 來搭配可數名詞。例如：There're eight people and only five burgers. We've got less burgers than we need.（這裏有八個人，但只有五個漢堡包。我們不夠漢堡包吃。）嚴格來説，這並不是規範英語，正確的説法應該是 fewer burgers。

fewer 和 less 的相反詞同樣是 more，表示數量上「更多的」，既可搭配可數名詞，也可搭配不可數名詞。例如：

- I've to make a few **more phone calls**. 我還得打多幾個電話。

- Would you like some **more tea**? 你要再來點茶嗎？

近字詞分清楚

❓ 詞語辨析

fit 作動詞用，意思是「合適」，表示衣物在尺寸、大小和剪裁上合適、合身。

suit 也是作動詞用，意思是「適合」，側重於表示衣服顏色、款式等符合你的口味，讓你變得好看。

⭐ 例句示範

fit

- My jeans don't **fit** me anymore!
  我的牛仔褲已經不合身了！

- This hat **fits** perfectly. I think I'll buy it.
  這頂帽子很貼合頭型——我想我會買下來。

suit

- You should wear blue more – it **suits** you.
  你應該多穿藍色的衣服——這個顏色很適合你。

- Jenny's new hairstyle doesn't really **suit** her.
  珍妮的新髮型不太適合她。

🔍 增潤知識

fit 也可作名詞用，指「適合；合身」。例如：

- This jacket is a perfect **fit**. 這件夾克十分合身。

還有一個與 fit 和 suit 容易混淆的動詞是 match。match 解作「與……相配」，指兩種顏色、設計或物品相配和相襯。例如：

- These shoes **match** these trousers.
  這雙鞋子很配這條褲子。

- Do you think this outfit **matches**?
  你認為這套衣服相襯嗎？

fun vs funny

意近字詞分清楚

❓ 詞語辨析

fun（拼寫結尾沒有 ny）作不可數名詞用，解作「樂趣；快樂；享受」。在口語中，亦可作形容詞用，解作「有趣的；令人愉快的」。

funny（拼寫結尾有 ny）作形容詞用，多用於口語中，解作「滑稽的；逗人笑的」，有時亦解作「古怪的；奇異的；難以解釋的」。

⭐ 例句示範

fun

- The children are having **fun** now.
  孩子正玩得開心。

- There are a lot of **fun** things to do in the park.
  在公園有很多有趣的事可以做。

- Try ice-skating – it's a really **fun** sport.
  試試溜冰吧——它真是個很好玩的運動。

funny

- Everybody laughed at his **funny** jokes.
  每個人聽到他的笑話都笑了。

- What's that **funny** smell?
  那是什麼怪味？

- I have a **funny** feeling something is going to happen.
  我有種奇怪的感覺，好像有什麼事情要發生了。

🔍 增潤知識

表示「令人愉快的」時，不要用 funny，而要用 fun。例如：

- The party was really **fun** and everyone enjoyed it.
  這個派對真的令人很開心，人人樂在其中。

意近字詞分清楚

❓ 詞語辨析

hear 作及物或不及物動詞用，指「聽到；聽見」。過去式和過去分詞都是 heard。

listen 作不及物動詞用，指「聽；傾聽」。若需要加上受詞，就必須在 listen 後面加上 to。

⭐ 例句示範

hear

- Speak up, please. I can't **hear** you.
  請說大聲點，我聽不到你的話。

- I **heard** the phone ring, but I couldn't find the phone.
  我聽到電話響，但我找不到電話。

- Grandpa doesn't **hear** too well anymore.
  爺爺聽得不太清楚了。

listen

- **Listen!** The birds are singing in the tree.
  聽一聽！樹上的鳥兒在唱歌。

- I love **listening to** music. 我喜歡聽音樂。

- You have to **listen** very carefully **to** the instructions.
  你要留心聽指示。

🔍 增潤知識

hear 和 listen 都有「聽」的意思，分別在於 hear 強調「不經意聽見」，listen 側重「專注地聆聽」。

hear 也可解作「聽說」。例如：

- I **heard** that your dad was ill. 我聽說你爸爸生病了。

漫畫看一看

意近字詞分清楚

❓ 詞語辨析

high 作形容詞用，指「高的」，尤指沒有生命的東西，強調事物本身離開地面很遠，例如飛機的飛行高度、山的高度。

tall 也作形容詞用，同樣指「高的」，可指人的身高，或指又窄又高的物件，強調人或物本身的高度，例如樹木。

⭐ 例句示範

high

- The **highest** mountain in Hong Kong is Tai Mo Shan.
  大帽山是香港最高的山。
- The bookshelf is too **high** for me to reach.
  書架太高，我碰不到。
- The castle was surrounded by **high** walls.
  城堡的四周圍着高牆。

tall

- I am 1.7 metre **tall**. 我身高一米七。
- James is much **taller** than his father.
  詹姆士比他的爸爸高得多。
- The office is in a **tall** building. 辦公室在一座高樓大廈裏。

🔍 增潤知識

high 和 tall 也有通用的時候，比如形容建築物時，我們可以説 a tall building 或 a high building，因為 building 這個字詞符合 high 和 tall 所使用的情形。

high 的名詞是 height。例如：

- He's about average **height**. 他大約中等個子。

invaluable vs valuable

漫畫看一看

Your help has been invaluable to me.

Are you saying my help is not valuable? You know how much work I've done for you!

No! On the contrary, your help is much needed. Here's a little present for you.

It looks valuable.

I hope you like it. I truly appreciate your help.

意近字詞分清楚

❓ 詞語辨析

invaluable（以 in 開頭）作形容詞用，意思是「寶貴的；極有用的」，強調的是作用。

valuable（開頭沒有 in）作形容詞用，意思是「貴重的；值錢的；有用的」，強調的是價錢。

⭐ 例句示範

invaluable

- The summer job provided us with **invaluable** experience.
  暑期工給我們帶來寶貴的經驗。
- The Internet is an **invaluable** source of information.
  互聯網是十分有用的資訊來源。

valuable

- He gave her a **valuable** necklace. 他送給她一條價值不菲的頸鏈。
- The museum has a fine collection of **valuable** paintings.
  這博物館收藏了很多珍貴名畫。

🔍 增潤知識

valuable 的相反詞不是 invaluable，而是 worthless（無價值的；不值錢的）。例如：

- They said her diamond ring was **worthless**.
  他們說她的鑽石戒指一文不值。

invaluable 和 valuable 都是從字根 value 衍生出來，指「價值」。例如：

- What is the **value** of this house? 這房子值多少錢？
- Your help has been of great **value**. 你的幫忙十分有用。

漫畫看一看

意近字詞分清楚

❓ 詞語辨析

lay 作動詞用，有兩個意思，一指「放置；安放」，二指「產卵；生蛋」，過去式和過去分詞是 laid，現在分詞是 laying。lay 也是動詞 lie（躺下）的過去式。

lie 作動詞用時，有兩個意思，第一個指「躺；平臥」，過去式是 lay，過去分詞是 lain，現在分詞是 lying。第二個意思指「說謊」，過去式和過去分詞是 lied，現在分詞是 lying。

⭐ 例句示範

lay

- He **laid** aside his schoolbag and went off.
  他把書包放在一邊，然後走去了。
- The hen **laid** three eggs. 母雞下了三隻蛋。

lie

- **Lie** down and rest for a while. 躺下來休息一會兒。
- She **lay** on her floor. 她躺在地板上。
- She **lied** to me. 她對我說謊。
- He's **lying**. I won't trust him anymore.
  他在撒謊，我不會再相信他。

🔍 增潤知識

慣用語 lay the table 指「擺好餐具，準備用餐」。例如：

- The food is ready – could you please **lay the table** for me?
  食物準備好了——你可以幫忙擺好餐具嗎？

lie 也可作名詞用，指「謊言」。例如：

- He told a **lie**. 他說了一個謊言。

❓ 詞語辨析

raise（拼寫中間有 a）指「舉起；抬起；提起」，也指「提高；增加」，作及物動詞用，後面必須有賓語。過去式和過去分詞都是 raised。

rise（拼寫中間沒有 a）指「（事物）升起」，或指「（人）站起」，也指「（數量或價值等）增加；增長」，作不及物動詞用，後面不能加賓語。過去式是 rose，過去分詞是 risen。

⭐ 例句示範

raise

- **Raise** your hand if you have any question.
  如有問題，請舉手。

- I can't hear you. Can you **raise** your voice a little bit?
  我聽不到你，你可以提高嗓門說話嗎？

- Many shops have **raised** their prices. 很多商店都加價了。

rise

- The balloons **rose** slowly into the sky.
  氣球慢慢升上天空。

- He **rose** from his chair to shake hands with us.
  他站起身和我們握手。

- House prices are **rising** all the time.
  房價一直在上漲。

🔍 增潤知識

慣用語 rise to your feet 指「站起」。例如：

- He **rose to his feet** when the teacher walked in.
  老師走進來時，他便站起身來。

漫畫看一看

Anna said she wanted to go to the cinema.

Is that so? She told me something different.

She said she wanted to stay at home. It's you who wanted to go to the cinema instead!

What did she tell you?

Oh, really? Never mind. It is said that this movie is very funny. Hope she will enjoy it.

❓ 詞語辨析

say 作動詞用，意思是「說；講」，過去式和過去分詞是 said。
say 後面可以直接加說話的具體內容或經過轉述的內容。

tell 作動詞用，意思是「告訴；說」，過去式和過去分詞是 told。
tell 後面可以直接加人稱代名詞的受格，再接說話的內容。

⭐ 例句示範

say

- Don't believe everything people **say** on the Internet.
  不要盡信人們在網絡上所說的話。

- "I'll see you later," Theo **said**. 「等會見。」西奧說。

- Peter **said** that he wanted to go to swim.
  彼得說他想去游泳。

tell

- **Tell** us the truth, please.
  請把真相告訴我們。

- Emma **told** me that she loves learning English.
  愛瑪跟我說她喜歡學英語。

🔍 增潤知識

say 和 tell 都有「說」的意思。雖然它們都可以用來引導說話的內容，但用法卻不同。

say 後面通常不加人稱代名詞，直接加某人的說話內容或經轉述的內容，即直接敘述句或間接敘述句。

而 tell 後面通常加上所告知對象或人稱代名詞受格，如 me、us、him 或 her。

sensible vs sensitive

❓ 詞語辨析

sensible（以 -ble 結尾）作形容詞用，指「理智的；明智的；合理的」，可以形容人或事物。

sensitive（以 -tive 結尾）作形容詞用，指「（人）敏感的；容易被冒犯的」或「（人）善解人意的；體貼的」，也指「（事情）敏感的；需要謹慎對待的」。

⭐ 例句示範

sensible

- We trust her because she is **sensible**.
  我們信任她，因為她很懂事。

- We have to make a **sensible** decision.
  我們必須作出明智的決定。

sensitive

- Wayne is very **sensitive** to criticism. 韋恩對批評很敏感。

- A good teacher is always **sensitive** to the needs of students.
  好教師總是能理解學生的需要。

- Sex education is still a **sensitive** issue in Hong Kong.
  在香港，性教育依然是敏感的話題。

🔍 增潤知識

sensible 和 sensitive 都是從字根 sense 衍生出來。

sense 有兩層意思，第一層意思是「感覺；感官（如視覺、聽覺、嗅覺、味覺和觸覺）」。例如：a sense of pride（自豪感）。

sense 第二層意思是「領悟；判斷力」。例如：

- This doesn't make **sense**. 這不合常理。

漫畫看一看

This robot can speak like human. He can speak different languages, too.

Really?

Yes, I do.

Yes. Talk to him. See how he responds.

Hello, what's your name?

My name is Robo. Nice to meet you!

意近字詞分清楚

❓ 詞語辨析

speak 作動詞用,指「說話」,主要用來表達說話的能力,可以是單向的。speak 既是及物又是不及物動詞,過去式是 spoke,過去分詞是 spoken。

talk 作動詞用,指「談話;討論」,主要用來表達聊天或交談,指雙向的溝通。由於 talk 是不及物動詞,所以後面要加上介詞 with、to 或 about。

⭐ 例句示範

speak

- Betty can't **speak** because she has a sore throat.
  貝蒂無法說話,因為她喉嚨痛。

- Calm down first. **Speak** slowly. 先冷靜下來,慢慢說。

- Do you **speak** Mandarin? 你會說普通話嗎?

talk

- Something's wrong here. We need to **talk**.
  有些地方出錯了,我們要談一下。

- Yoyo looks very sad. Go **talk** to her.
  瑤瑤看來很傷心,去跟她聊聊吧。

🔍 增潤知識

speak 和 talk 都有「說話」的意思。在一些情況,例如表達講述某事時,兩者是互通的。例如:

- She **spoke** / **talked** about her hobbies. 她在說自己的嗜好。

- Don't interrupt me when I'm **speaking** / **talking**.
  我說話時不要打斷我。

練習室 1

There is a mistake in each of the following sentences. Strike them through and correct them in the spaces provided.

下列句子均有一處錯誤，請刪去錯誤的部分，並在橫線上寫上正確答案。

範例	Uncle Pang is very ~~high~~.	tall
1	~~Lie~~ the pens on the table, please.	
2	This skirt ~~suits~~ you perfectly.	
3	This reservoir has ~~fewer~~ water than that one.	
4	Everyone was invited to the party ~~accept~~ Mary.	
5	Do you play other sports ~~beside~~ badminton?	
6	Would you like some ~~desert~~?	
7	Could you ~~take~~ me some water?	
8	I ~~lent~~ a novel from the library yesterday.	
9	~~Its~~ so nice of you to invite us!	
10	My bag was ~~opened~~ and my wallet was gone!	

參考答案：1. Lie → Lay　2. suits → fits　3. fewer → less　4. accept → except
5. beside → besides　6. desert → dessert　7. take → bring
8. lent → borrowed　9. Its → It's　10. opened → open

130

練習室 2

Fill in the blanks with the correct word for the following sentences. Change the word form if necessary.

請為下列句子填寫正確的字詞，並按需改變字詞的詞形。

範例

adapt / adopt

They've ____adopted____ a baby boy.

It took me a while to ____adapt____ to the new job.

waist / waste

1a. What a complete _____ of time!

1b. The jeans are too tight around my _____ .

flea / flee

2a. Many people have _____ their homes because of war.

2b. Are you sure the kitten has _____ ?

sweat / sweet

3a. We were dripping with _____ after running.

3b. She bought a packet of _____ .

aisle / isle

4a. Would you prefer a window or an _____ seat?

4b. Can you find _____ of Wight on the map?

pray / prey

5a. Let's _____ for the victims of the earthquake.

5b. The tiger is stalking its _____ .

參考答案：1a. waste 1b. waist 2a. fled 2b. fleas 3a. sweat 3b. sweets 4a. aisle 4b. isle 5a. pray 5b. prey

練習室 3

Write the correct letter in the spaces provided to complete the following sentences. One of the letters will be used more than once.

請在橫線上填寫正確的字母，以完成下列句子。其中一個字母會使用多於一次。

A diary **B** dairy **C** daily **D** lastly **E** lately **F** later **G** latter **H** last **I** late

範例	I have a lot of things to write in the ___A___ today.
1	I haven't seen my cousins _____.
2	He is a famous director. Have you watched his _____ film?
3	I'd like to thank Ann, Dora, Jessie, and, _____, my parents.
4	Exercise has become part of my _____ routine.
5	You will find all the yogurts in the _____ section.
6	I'm busy right now. I'll call you _____ on.
7	The Visitor Centre is open _____ between 9 a.m. and 6 p.m.
8	You can go there either by taxi or bus . The _____ costs less.
9	"I swear this is the _____ cigarette I will ever smoke, " he said.
10	I have kept a _____ on and off since I was six.

練習室4

Choose the correct word for the following sentences.
Tick the correct box.

請為下列句子選擇正確的字詞，並在 ☐ 內加 ✔ 。

範例 They were injured in a car (✔ A. accident ☐ B. incident).

1 The bad (☐ A. weather ☐ B. whether) did not stop them from having a good time.

2 He got a sunburn from (☐ A. laying ☐ B. lying) on the beach too long.

3 By the time I saw her, she had already (☐ A. past ☐ B. passed) me.

4 Everyone knows that (☐ A. its ☐ B. it's) her fault.

5 I saw his face (☐ A. between ☐ B. among) the crowd.

6 I will try not to let their words (☐ A. affect ☐ B. effect) me.

7 We hurried to the station, but the train had (☐ A. all ready ☐ B. already) left.

8 A cheesecake's (☐ A. principal ☐ B. principle) ingredients are cream cheese and sugar.

9 At the assembly, the (☐ A. principal ☐ B. principle) introduced each guest speaker.

0 I don't want any (☐ A. further ☐ B. farther) explanation.

Use the correct word from the list below to complete the following sentences.

請從下表選擇正確的字詞，以完成下列句子。

lose	lost	loose	tough
though	thorough	through	thought

範例　Don't _____ lose _____ my keys.

1　I _____ he was a liar, so I turned him down.

2　The little boy looks _____. Shall we help him?

3　_____ they are poor, they are happy.

4　If you _____ the ticket, you won't be able to get into the cinema.

5　The thieves got in _____ the window.

6　Clothes that are _____ are quite comfortable.

7　The police made a _____ search of the building.

8　This meat is _____. I don't want to eat it.

參考答案：1. thought 2. lost 3. Though 4. lose 5. through 6. loose 7. thorough 8. tough

練習室 6

There are nine mistakes in the text below. Circle and correct them in the spaces provided.

以下文章有九處錯誤，請圈起錯誤部分，並在橫線上寫上正確答案。

Denzel had never studied (aboard) before. When he first came to the US, he felt very alone. He felt boring, too, because he had no friends. He missed his family in Kenya everyday.

One day, when Denzel was wondering around the city, some boys threw stones towards him. They were his schoolmates. They made funny of Denzel because of his skin colour. Since then, he became very sensible about his skin colour. He video chatted with Lakin, his best friend in his hometown. Lakin adviced him to talk to a teacher or an adult he trusted.

Denzel then wrote down what he would like to say in an email and sent it to his teacher. The teacher took immediate action. "We don't tolerate bullying! You guys simply lack sympathy to others!" the teacher said. The bullies learnt their lessons and apologised to Denzel. At the end of the school term, Denzel was awarded a metal for his bravery to stand up to bullies.

列	abroad	⑤	_____
	_____	⑥	_____
	_____	⑦	_____
	_____	⑧	_____
	_____	⑨	_____

趣味漫畫學英語

小學漫畫英語王：Easily Confused Words 易混淆詞

作　　者：Aman Chiu
繪　　圖：黃裳
責任編輯：黃稔茵
美術設計：劉麗萍
出　　版：新雅文化事業有限公司
　　　　　香港英皇道 499 號北角工業大廈 18 樓
　　　　　電話：(852) 2138 7998
　　　　　傳真：(852) 2597 4003
　　　　　網址：http://www.sunya.com.hk
　　　　　電郵：marketing@sunya.com.hk
發　　行：香港聯合書刊物流有限公司
　　　　　香港荃灣德士古道 220-248 號荃灣工業中心 16 樓
　　　　　電話：(852) 2150 2100
　　　　　傳真：(852) 2407 3062
　　　　　電郵：info@suplogistics.com.hk
印　　刷：中華商務彩色印刷有限公司
　　　　　香港新界大埔汀麗路 36 號
版　　次：二〇二三年七月初版

ISBN: 978-962-08-8245-6